I'd Rather Be A
dragon

KATIE NEWELL

I'd Rather Be A Dragon
Copyright © 2016 by Katie Newell

Published in the United States by:

Credo House Publishers,
a division of Credo Communications, LLC,
Grand Rapids, Michigan
www.credohousepublishers.com

Fieldstone Press, LLC
Lowell, Michigan
www.fieldstonepress.com

ISBN: 978-1-625860-54-5

Cover and interior by Katie Newell
Edited by Donna Huisjen

Printed in the United States of America
First edition

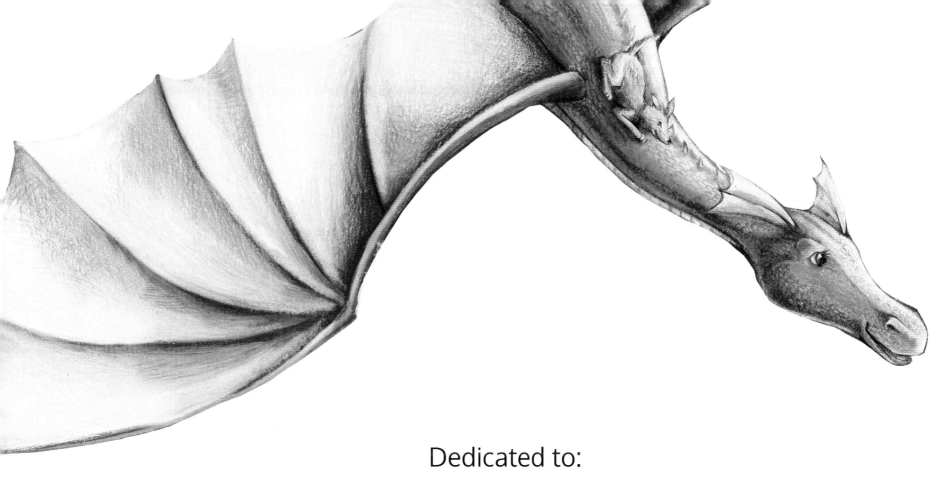

Dedicated to:

H., C., & A.

You're the best dragons a mom could ask for.

- K. N.

I don't dream
of being a princess.

It takes far too long to brush my hair.

There's always mud between my toes,

and running in a fancy gown is impossible.

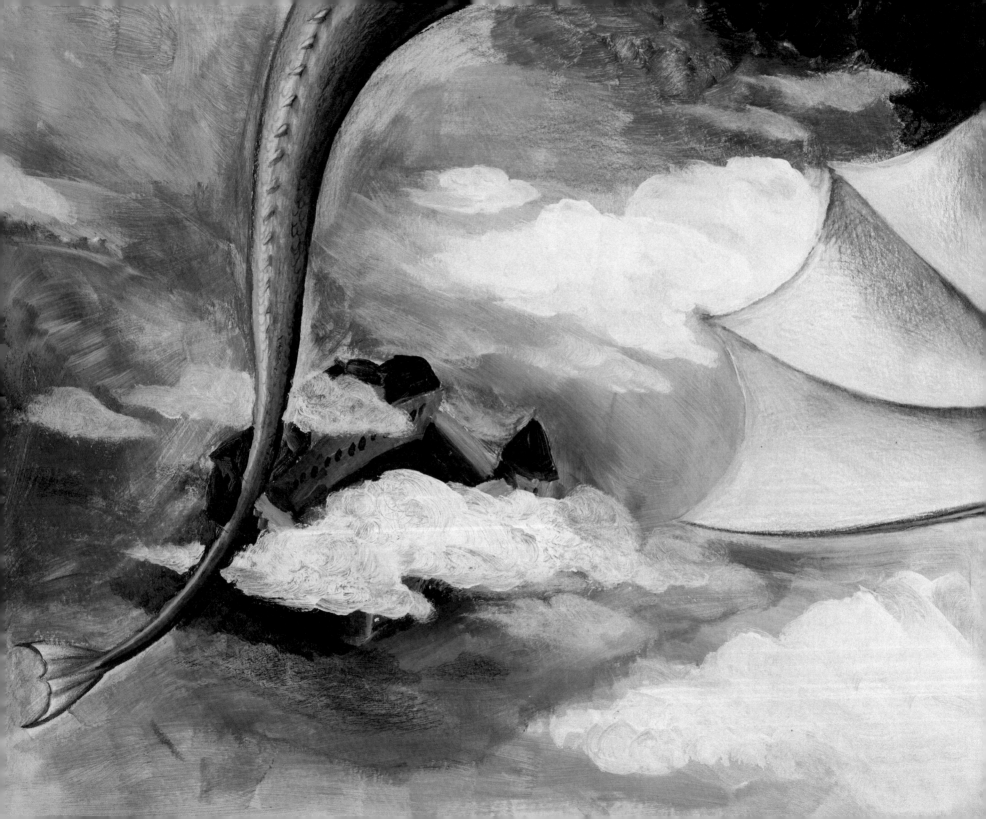

I'd rather be a dragon.

I would tumble in the breeze,
play tag with the birds,
and, of course, breathe fire.

I'm too clumsy for tea parties.

I've accidently knocked cupcakes on the floor,

spilled tea on the table,

and even broke my cup.

I would rather go exploring.

I'd hike under emerald trees,
run free through grassy fields,
and catch frogs
from sunrise to sunset.

My friends love to play dress-up.

They try on hats decorated with feathers,
long pink dresses that shimmer,
and short purple dresses that sparkle.

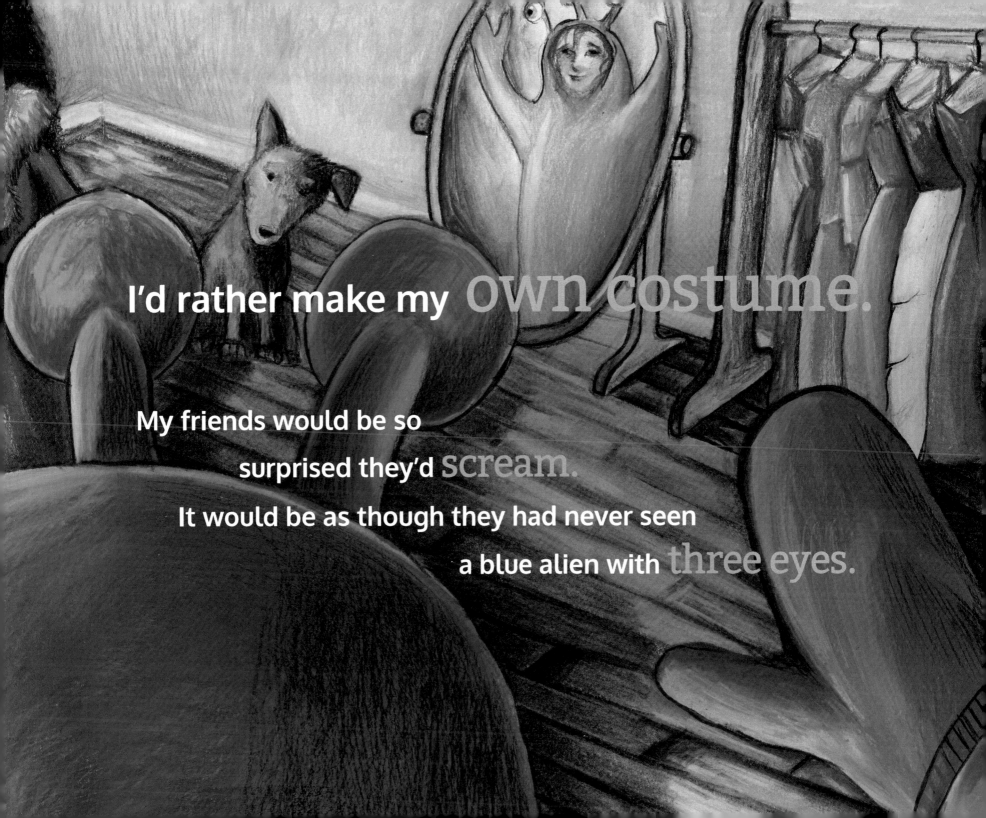

I'd rather make my own costume.

My friends would be so surprised they'd scream. It would be as though they had never seen a blue alien with three eyes.

I'm absolutely terrible at dancing.

My feet have a mind of their own:

I turn left instead of right,

and I never can remember all the moves.

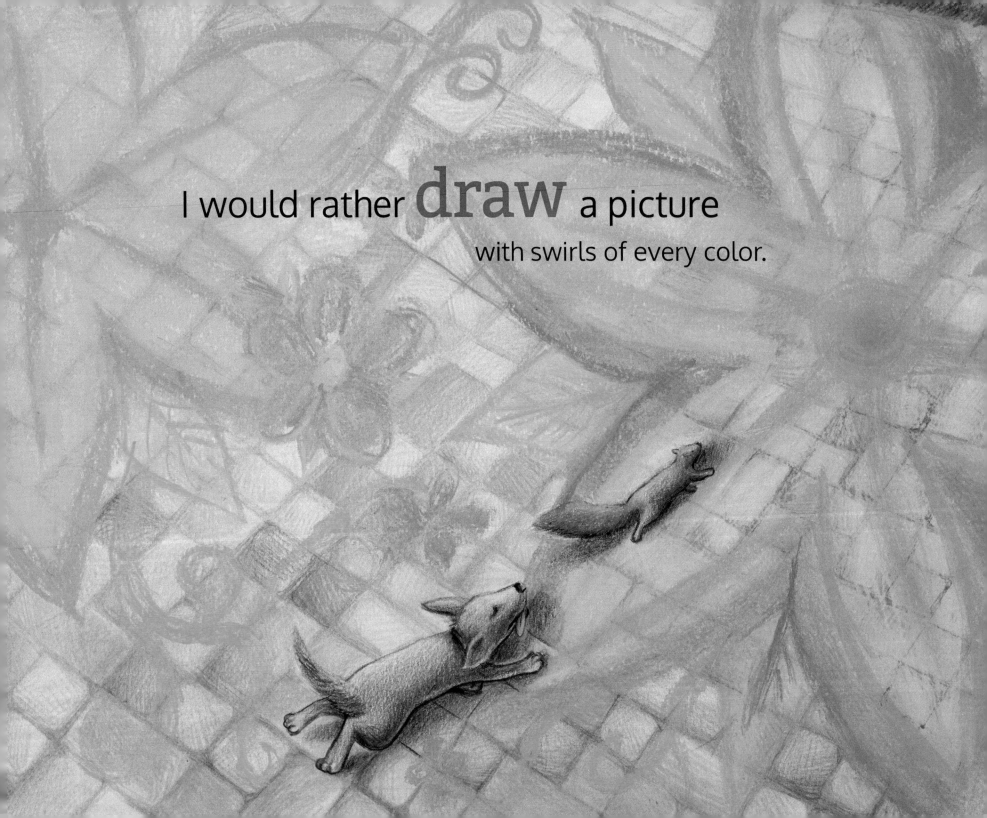

I would rather **draw** a picture with swirls of every color.

Each line would be a dance
that came alive out of my hands.

I'm always looking for lost homework.

I'll check under my bed,
in the bathtub,
in the trash,
and in the dog's bowl.
It's never anywhere to be found.

Once I helped **bake a cake.**

I thought I had mixed the ingredients just right—
until we put it in the oven
and it **started to inflate** like a balloon.

Right now I would rather go 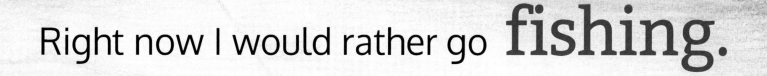 fishing.

I'll spend the afternoon on the dock,

catching fish for dinner.

But this time

I'll leave the cooking to someone else.

When everyone's headed one way

I seem to be going the other.

When everyone sees one thing

I see something completely different.

Sometimes I worry

that I don't quite fit in.

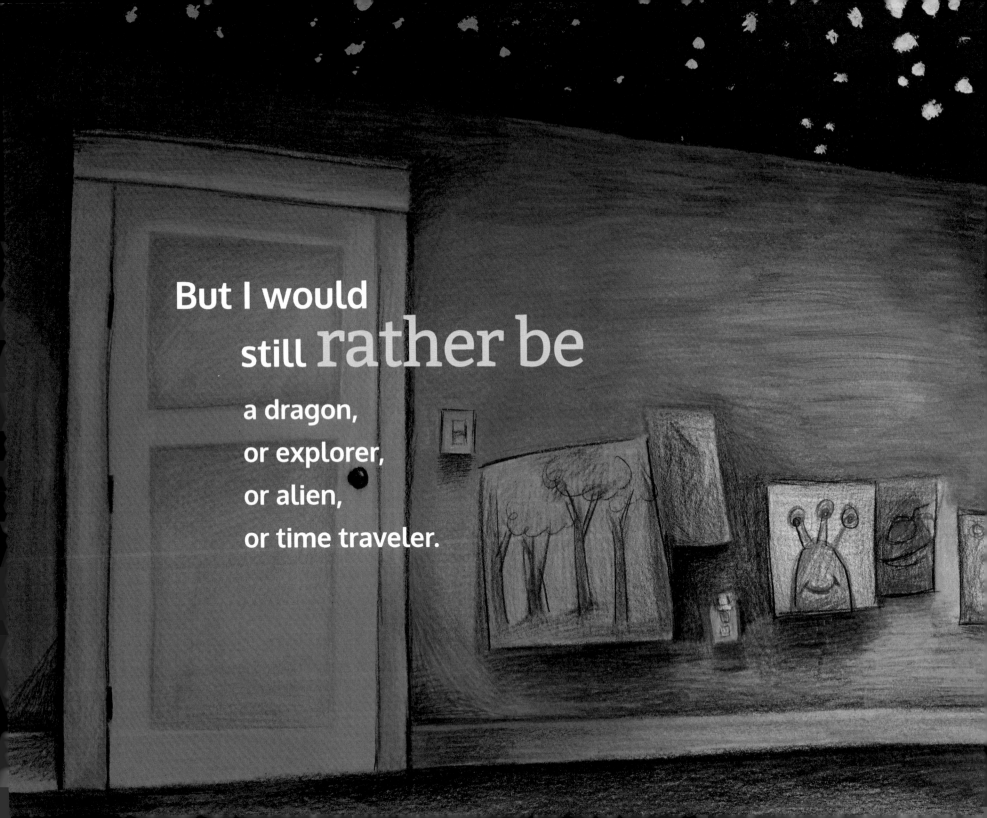

But I would
still rather be

a dragon,
or explorer,
or alien,
or time traveler.